What I Saw in the Teachers' Lounge

by Jerry Pallotta

Cartwheel Books
An Imprint of Scholastic Inc.

Illustrated by
Howard McWilliam

I saw Ann Stearns and Nancy Howard
in the teachers' lounge.
—J.P.

For little Rufus, with love
—H.W.

Text copyright © 2012 by Jerry Pallotta
Illustrations copyright © 2012 by Howard McWilliam

All rights reserved. Published by Scholastic Inc.
SCHOLASTIC, CARTWHEEL BOOKS, and associated logos are trademarks
and/or registered trademarks of Scholastic Inc.
ISBN: 978-0-545-38473-5

12 11 10 9 8 7 6 5 4   15 16 17 18

Printed in the USA   40
First printing, September 2014

I saw the sign on the door at school every day.

It wasn't fair.
Why couldn't students go in there?

Oops—the door was open.
I thought I'd take a peek.

The first time I looked, I saw my teacher.

She was surfing.

Another teacher was in full hiking gear.

She was climbing
a rugged mountain.

I took another look. The whole staff was scuba diving.

Yikes! One teacher almost got eaten by a shark.

I looked in the corner
of the lounge.

Some teachers were skiing.
The snow was perfect.

In the school cafeteria, we ate lunch.

In the teachers' lounge, they had
frog-eyeball soup, snake-brain pizza,
and elephant-toenail cupcakes.

I wondered what they tasted like.

After lunch, I peeked again.

My gym teacher was wrestling a grizzly bear.

Other teachers went for a walk in the rain forest.

They were surrounded by pretty birds.

I told my classmates everything.
They thought I was fibbing.

No one believed
a word I said. . . .

When they looked in the
teachers' lounge, nothing happened.
Everything was normal.

I peeked again.

The teachers were riding camels.

They were shopping in a market.

The kindergarten teachers
rode over to the pyramids.

I wished I could go in
the teachers' lounge.

I saw one
teacher fishing.

Other teachers were
digging for clams and
pulling lobster traps.

Don't move! Watch out!
Now the teachers were on a safari.

I saw a lion. Over there were a cheetah and some hyenas.

I watched one teacher feed a killer whale while water-skiing.

Just then, the principal walked by.

"Get back to class," he said. "Stop peeking in the teachers' lounge."

I want to be a teacher when I grow up.